NOCTILA
THE DEATH OWL

BY ADAM BLADE

ORCHARD

So... You still wish to follow Tom on his Beast Quest.

Turn back now. A great evil lurks beneath Avantia, waiting to arise and conquer the kingdom with violence and rage. Six Beasts with the hearts of Ancient Warriors, at the mercy of the Evil Wizard, Malvel, who I fear has reached the height of his powers.

War awaits us all.

I beg you again: Close this book and turn away. Evil will rise. Darkness will fall.

Your friend,
Wizard Aduro

PROLOGUE

A prison of cold, blue fire surrounded Malvel.

He sat alone in his chamber, in the tallest turret of his ruined castle. The walls had collapsed in his years of absence, leaving a jagged hole like a mouth of rotting teeth. Malvel stared out over the barren landscape of Gorgonia.

Red clouds swirled above the endless plains. No one dared approach the castle, even now.

The Evil Wizard had lost track of the days and nights since he'd found himself back here. He'd come so close to burning the Warlock's Staff in the Eternal Flame of Seraph. If he had managed to do that, he'd have achieved ultimate power – he would have had the strength to conquer any kingdom he wished.

But he'd failed. One moment he'd been fighting, and the next he'd fallen into the Flame itself.

And all because of that wretched boy...

"Tom!" He spat the name of his enemy.

It was over. While the fiery cage encased him, Malvel could never leave his castle, never step foot in Avantia again. Only one man had the spells to release him – Good Wizard

Aduro. Malvel scoffed. *And why should that old fool help me?*

But Malvel had set a plan in motion so that was starting to happen back in Avantia…

A dust cloud had appeared on the horizon. Malvel narrowed his eyes and saw a rider galloping across the plain towards the castle.

"A visitor?" he muttered.

The horse carried a soldier wearing armour, but Malvel wasn't afraid. No weapon known to man could penetrate the magical flames that surrounded him.

He heard the horse enter the castle grounds, and then the slow tread of footsteps climbing the stone stairs. He turned to the doorway as a figure stepped from the shadows. The armoured man still wore his helmet.

"You show great courage trespassing here," said Malvel. "Foolish courage."

The intruder lifted a gauntleted hand, unclipped the fastenings behind his helmet, and pulled it away.

Long red locks tumbled free.

"Freya!" gasped Malvel.

Tom's mother walked slowly around him, her hand on the hilt of her sword. "Aduro told me I'd find you here," she said.

"How is my old enemy?" sneered Malvel. "Sent you to check up on me, has he?"

"I was returning from Gwildor," Freya replied. "Aduro used his magic to send me here. You've harmed Avantia for the last time."

Malvel gestured to the blue flames around him. "You're wrong. I've made sure of that."

Freya's brow creased. "What are you talking about?" she said.

Malvel smiled. "New evil is coming to Avantia. An ancient magic destined to destroy that petty kingdom and kill your son."

"You're lying,' said Freya, but Malvel could see the fear in her eyes.

"Let me show you," he said, grinning wider. He lifted both hands so his palms faced each another. Between them formed a ball of yellow flame. An image came into focus within the orb, showing peaceful villages dotting a beautiful landscape. Animals roamed in green fields under clear blue skies.

"Is that...?" Freya began.

"Avantia?" Malvel said. "Yes – my precious home. Are you watching closely?"

Suddenly a black shape fell over the kingdom and Freya jerked back in horror. Malvel grinned to himself as a giant Beast shaped like an owl swooped over the fields, scattering terrified cattle. The vision followed its soaring journey, its orange eyes aglow. Grey feathers dripped with thick black tar, leaving a trail of fire through a field of crops, scorching them to blackened stumps.

The Beast opened its beak to reveal jagged teeth set in bleeding red gums. It screeched, making Freya clutch her ears.

As the image faded, a cold wind swept into the ruined turret, but Malvel didn't feel the cold at all.

"What *is* that thing?" asked Freya, her voice trembling.

"Meet Noctila," said Malvel. "The new enemy of Avantia."

CHAPTER ONE

FALLING DARKNESS

The arrow *thwacked* into the bullseye of the target and the crowd of servants cheered. Elenna blushed and gave a little bow. Beside her, Silver howled with delight.

"Show-off," said Tom, smiling at his friend. "Perhaps you should move it a bit closer for everyone else."

Elenna laughed. "I'm sure there'll be plenty of people better than me."

They'd been at King Hugo's palace since dawn, helping to set up the courtyard for the Summer Solstice celebrations that evening. Every summer the people of Avantia gathered to celebrate the longest day of the year and Elenna was in charge of the archery competition.

"Help me move this," Tom said, bracing himself at one end of a long trestle table.

Elenna slung her bow over her shoulder. She took the other end of the table and they heaved it into position alongside the others to form a horseshoe shape around the edge of the courtyard. King Hugo would be seated at the head, and all his courtiers around him. There would be benches for all the villagers in the middle and festivities would spill out into the rest of the palace grounds.

One of the cooks had told Tom about last year's celebration with a glow in her eyes. By the time dusk fell, torches would be lit around the walls and the tables would be laden with food from the palace kitchens and the surrounding villages: huge wheels of cheese, roasted meat and fowl of every kind, fruits and vegetables and fine pastries. Tom could already smell the bread baking in the palace oven, and his mouth watered.

"My Uncle Leo's coming along later," said Elenna. "It's been so long since…"

"Help!" called a voice.

Elenna rushed over to steady the base of a tottering ladder. At the top a stable boy was trying to tie a stream of bunting over the portcullis.

"Thank you!" he called down.

Elsewhere, musicians were practising a jig for the dancing that would follow the feast.

Tom ruffled Silver's neck. He knew he should be happy like everyone else, but he couldn't drive the worry from his heart.

Almost two days had passed since he and Elenna had returned from the magical kingdom of Seraph. They'd defeated the six Beasts Malvel had sent against them, and they'd rescued the Warlock's Staff before it could be burned in the Eternal Flame. If they'd failed, Aduro would have died and Malvel would now be ruling all the kingdoms. Tom shivered at the thought.

On returning to Avantia, the flush

of triumph had quickly cooled.
When Tom had told Aduro that the
Eternal Flame had consumed Malvel,
the Wizard's face had turned pale.
He'd told Tom that Malvel wasn't
dead at all, but even more powerful
than ever.

The clapping of a group of stable
boys shook Tom from his thoughts.

He saw the bunting was finally in place. Elenna smiled over and he tried to grin back. The Summer Solstice was always one of the happiest times in Avantia. As well as archery and feasting, there'd be tests of strength, apple bobbing and Tom's favourite – the steeplechase around the castle walls.

Tom wished his parents could be here, but Aduro had sent both Freya and Taladon on missions in foreign kingdoms. He said it was just a precaution, but Tom suspected it had something to do with Malvel.

A red-faced maidservant bustled towards Tom carrying a basket full of tablecloths.

"Master Tom," she sighed. "These have been eaten through by moths. It'll take all day to repair them.

I thought that perhaps the King's Wizard might help. If Master Tom would put in a word…"

Tom took the basket from her. "Of course. Leave it with me. I'm sure Aduro has a spell that can fix them."

The maid thanked him and curtseyed. As Tom turned back towards the palace, Elenna joined him. "Why didn't she take them herself?" she asked.

"I think we both know why," said Tom. "Let's go up and see him."

He frowned as they entered the cool staircase that spiralled up to the Wizard's chamber. Aduro hadn't been the same since they'd returned from Seraph. He looked tired all the time, his temper was short and he was always snapping at his apprentice, Daltec.

They reached the heavy chamber door, and Elenna knocked. There was no answer. Elenna knocked again. Tom heard the sound of shuffling from inside. He shared a concerned look with Elenna then slowly pushed open the creaking door.

A wave of stale air drifted over them. The shutters were drawn across the windows, casting the room in a gloomy pall. A single lit candle sputtered on the wall. Aduro sat hunched in the far corner, his cloak hugged tight to his body. His grey hair, greasy and unkempt, trailed over his shoulders. His hands cradled his crystal ball and he stared at its gleaming surface.

Tom placed the basket on the ground. "Aduro?"

The Wizard turned his tired eyes

slowly towards them. Shadows sat in
the hollows of his cheeks. "When the
sun sets tonight," muttered Aduro,
"it may never rise again. Eternal
darkness will fall."

Tom crouched in front of the
Wizard, but Aduro was already
gazing at the ball again.

"What are you talking about?" asked Tom.

Aduro trailed his fingers across the crystal. "A powerful evil,' he groaned. "I see it only faintly."

"Whatever it is," said Tom, "we'll face it—"

With a grinding of stone, the room shook violently, throwing Tom and Elenna onto their backs and sending Aduro's crystal ball rolling across the ground. Tom staggered to the shutters. Gripping the window frame with one hand, Tom threw them open.

Outside, beyond the palace walls, screaming men and women ran. A huge section of the road leading to the front of the castle had collapsed, and cracks spread out into the surrounding fields. A cart had toppled, spilling barrels across the cobbles. A horse reared and threw its rider.

"We have to do something!" said Elenna.

Tom heard a scuffle behind him, and turned to see Aduro scrambling to his feet and rushing through the door. "Wait for us!" he said.

Casting a final glance out of the window, he saw grey clouds sweeping the blue sky aside.

Perhaps Aduro's right, Tom thought. *Perhaps darkness is coming after all.* He turned from the window. "Come on," he cried. "After Aduro!"

CHAPTER TWO

THE PAST AWAKENS

They stood on the edge of the sunken crater just beyond the castle walls. The fallen cart had been righted, and Captain Harkman's soldiers had ushered the bystanders away. Tom stared into the black abyss.

"This was no ordinary earthquake," said Aduro. He raised his hands to form a white glowing orb and then launched it like a dove. It sailed down into the darkness, casting rays of light into the gloom.

Tom gasped as he saw stone carvings of swords and shields, armour and the shapes of terrible Beasts. He'd seen this place before, when they'd faced Mortaxe the Skeleton Warrior.

"It's the Gallery of Tombs!" he said.

Aduro nodded gravely. "That's right. But no one has seen this part for hundreds of years."

As the ball of light drifted over the wreckage, Tom counted six marble tombs in a row. The lids had been cracked open. Tom frowned as he noticed something strange. Instead of caving in, pieces of the lids had scattered outwards.

"They were broken open from

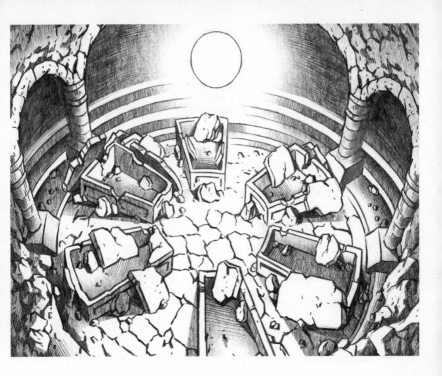

the inside!" Tom gasped.

"Who was buried in them?" asked Elenna nervously.

Aduro was silent and when Tom turned to face him, he was shocked to see the Wizard smiling.

"Old allies," said Aduro. "Look." He pointed towards the horizon, and with a click of his fingers conjured a smoky vision. The soldiers who guarded the crater muttered in alarm and the bystanders gasped and pointed. The image inside seemed to bring the far distance into close focus, and over the fields Tom saw a perfectly straight line of six knights in full, brightly coloured armour: red, blue, silver, black, white and gold. Incredibly, even wearing heavy metal plates, they were running.

"Are they even human?" Tom asked.

"They were once," said Aduro. "They're the Knights of Forton. Six ancient defenders of the kingdom given mystical powers. They fought alongside the very first Master of the Beasts."

"Tanner?" said Tom, remembering that Aduro had mentioned his name the last time they'd visited the Gallery of Tombs.

"The Knights were laid to rest over

three hundred years ago," said Aduro.

"But why have they been awakened now?" asked Tom.

The Good Wizard's smile faded. "Legend says they will rise when Avantia faces its darkest hour."

Pride spread through Tom's chest. "Whatever Malvel is planning, we'll be ready with the Knights of Forton at our side."

But when he turned back to Aduro, the Wizard was staring into the sunken crater. The glowing orb rested over what looked like a huge chest made of dragon-hide. It had also been violently opened, creating jagged, leathery edges.

"No! It can't be!" gasped Aduro.

"What is it?" asked Elenna. She scrambled down the slope.

Tom followed with Aduro. The dust

was still settling from the earthquake, and the ground crunched beneath every step. Tom saw the dragon-tomb was painted with crude silver and gold images of Beasts. One looked like an owl, one a cheetah, another seemed to be covered in dripping moss. There was a strange octopus with two heads, and something like a giant armadillo. Last of all was a lion with the head of a skeleton and a mane of golden flames. The images sent a shudder through Tom.

"What are they?" he asked.

Aduro wrung his hands together. "If my books are correct, these are the Beasts the Knights of Forton defeated," he said. "This chest stored their bones."

Elenna peered through the hole. "It's empty now."

Tom saw Aduro swallow thickly. "Then somehow Malvel has found a way to bring them back."

"Wait!" said Elenna. "There is something inside!" She seized the broken edges of the dragon hide and began to pull, but she couldn't open it further.

"Stand aside," said Tom, drawing his sword. With a few well-aimed hacks, he succeeded in cutting away a panel of the chest. The interior was the dark scarlet colour of dried dragon flesh. Inside were six small objects.

The first was a net of spun silver, then a piece of orange amber. Beside that lay a silver spinning disc, and a miniature ship's harpoon. Next was a tooth the size of Tom's fist, serrated along its edges and broken off across the root. Last of all was a gleaming dart. Tom reached out and touched it.

35

"It's cold!" he gasped. "An icicle!"

"Magic has preserved it," said Aduro. "These are the six tokens that the Knights used to defeat their Beast enemies. If Malvel has brought these Beasts back to life, the Knights will need them."

"I'll find the Knights and return the tokens!" said Tom.

"If evil threatens Avantia, they'll need our help," said Elenna.

Aduro gave them a thin smile. "Your bravery does you credit. Here." With a swish of his hand, a canvas bag appeared beside the objects. Tom scooped them inside and hitched the bag over his shoulder.

"Are those Varkules?" asked Elenna, pointing further into the wrecked Gallery.

Tom followed her gaze and saw six

giant hyena-like creatures staring from a carving in the wall. They had sharp, deadly looking tusks sprouting from their lower jaws. "My uncle used to tell me stories about them."

"They're nothing to worry about," said Aduro. "Varkules were vicious creatures, bred by evil men to terrify the people of Avantia. The Knights of Forton found a litter of cubs and tamed them. But they've been dead for hundreds of years."

The Wizard held out his hand, and the light orb flew back into his palm.

Its surface dulled to a swirling pattern of white marble, etched with dark lines. It took Tom a moment to realise the lines formed into a map of Avantia.

"Take this with you," said Aduro, a flicker of excitement sparking in his eyes. "It will help you to follow the Knights of Forton."

As Tom looked, the snaking tracks of the Knights split into two, then four, then six.

"They're all heading in different directions," said Elenna.

"That's very strange," Aduro said. "You must be careful. I sense things aren't as simple as they seem."

Just as Tom was tucking the globe into his canvas bag with the magical tokens, another earthquake shook the ground. Tom and Elenna clutched one another to stay standing as the remains of the tombs crumbled and collapsed around them. Above, the crowds who stood at the edge of the crater screamed and backed away.

Tom's saw movement high on the wall. Chips of stone flaked off the Varkule carvings, then chunks of rock. Tom thought he saw fur breaking through where one of the forelegs had been.

"Aduro..." he began.

As the shaking stilled, he heard several growls fill the air. A striped muzzle pushed through the stone. A Varkule pulled itself free from the carving, and shook the dust from its thick, spotted fur. Drool spilled from its black lips, and its yellow claws rattled against the ground. Two eyes fell upon Tom and Elenna, narrowing to slits. It was going to attack!

CHAPTER THREE

EVIL SPREADS

The creature pounced. Tom lifted his shield and felt the paws slam into him. He sprawled across the ground, his nostrils filled with the hot stink of the creature's fur. As soon as Tom's hand found the hilt of his sword, the Varkule had vanished. Elenna came rushing to his side.

"Are you all right?" she asked.

Tom climbed unsteadily to his

feet, just in time to see the last of the snarling, snapping Varkules disappearing over the brow of the crater. Tom ran up the slope after them as the soldiers scattered in fear.

"There's no point!" Aduro called. "They didn't want to kill you."

Tom stopped, breathing heavily. "I can't let them go – they'll be a danger to innocent people."

"You have bigger battles to face," said the Wizard. "Besides, a Varkule runs faster than any horse."

Tom watched the giant hyenas streaming across the fields in the same direction as the Knights. "I thought you said they were tame!"

"They were once," said Aduro. "Malvel's magic must have twisted their natures, which worries me…"

"Why?" asked Elenna.

"Never mind," said Aduro. He sat heavily on the edge of a broken tomb and buried his head in his hands.

Tom had never seen Aduro look so defeated. He strode to the Wizard's side and took his arm. "Listen to me," he said. "Return to the palace and try to keep the people calm. Tell the King…"

"Tell the King what?" said a voice above. "What was that thing I saw running away?"

Tom saw King Hugo descending into the shattered Gallery of Tombs.

"The kingdom is being threatened by Malvel again," said Elenna. "The creature you saw was a Varkule."

"Malvel?" said Hugo. "I thought he was gone for good."

"We don't have time to explain," said Tom. "We need to round up Storm and Silver and get moving.

There are Beasts to face, and
we'll defeat them, including those
Varkules. Await word from us here."

The King nodded, and helped
Aduro to his feet.

Tom turned to Elenna. "While
there's blood in my veins, Avantia
will not fall to Malvel's curse."

Tom spurred Storm hard with Elenna
in the saddle behind him. The stallion
responded with a burst of speed.
He'd been stabled for several weeks
and seemed to enjoy the hard ride
away from the City and across the
Grassy Plains. The canvas bag with the
ancient artefacts was tied tight to his
saddle. Silver had been keen to go too,
running excited circles around Elenna.

"According to the globe map, the

Silver Knight is nearest," Tom called over his shoulder to his friend. "We should find him first."

The trail led them towards the northeastern edge of the Forest of Fear and the village of Lorrinel. There were questions that kept swirling around Tom's head. Why had the Knights run away like that? Why hadn't they stopped to speak to Aduro?

They entered the main street of Lorrinel. It was the day of the Summer Solstice, so he expected the villagers here, like those nearer King Hugo's castle, to be out celebrating. But the stalls along the edges of the road had been overturned. Bunting was trodden into the dirt, and all the houses lining the streets were bolted closed, with their window hatches tightly shut. A dog cowered beside a well.

"We're too late," Elenna whispered.

Tom thought he saw a pair of eyes
staring through an open window,
but they quickly vanished. An eerie
silence lay over the village. The
thatched roof of the Market Hall
was crushed on one side, and the
tables of food still standing had been
abandoned to the flies.

"Water…" groaned a voice. "Help…"

Tom slipped out of the saddle, and tracked the calls. Elenna followed, leading Storm by his reins.

"I can't see where it's coming from," Tom said.

Elenna beckoned to Silver. "Find him," she muttered to the wolf.

Silver immediately lowered his nose to the ground and darted off. Tom broke into a jog.

On the far side of the Market Hall, Silver led them to a toppled table. At first all Tom saw was a pair of legs, but after heaving the table away, he found an elderly man, his arm twisted awkwardly across his body. His clothes were torn to bloody shreds.

"Bless you!" he mumbled.
"I thought I would not survive."

Elenna fished out a water flask from

Storm's saddlebag and held it to the man's lips. He slurped thirstily. When he'd finished, he managed to sit up, wincing. He nodded to his arm. "I think it's broken."

"Stay still a moment," said Tom. He detached Skor's jewel from his belt and held it above the man's arm.

Gradually, a smile spread over his face. "That's amazing," he said, flexing his wrist. Tom healed the worst of his cuts and then he and Elenna helped the man to stand.

"What happened here?" Tom asked.

The old man's eyes widened. "It was horrible. The whole village was enjoying the festivities when the monster came. I heard screams and shouts of fear. People were running for their lives. The next thing I know, the ground shook and the table where I was sitting seemed to leap into the air. People were shouting, 'Monster! Monster!'. Then there was a crack and a wooden beam fell on me. I didn't see any more."

"A monster? It must have been one of the Varkules," Elenna whispered.

Tom nodded and faced the man again. "Tell the people of the village to stay inside. There could be more of these creatures about and we mean to stop them."

The old man cast his watery eyes up and down Tom, then to Elenna and Silver. His glance lingered for a moment on Tom's sword. "What can two children and a wolf do about that monster?"

Tom seized Storm's reins and climbed into the saddle. Elenna vaulted up behind him. As they trotted away, she called back. "Trust us!"

CHAPTER FOUR

A BATTLE IN THE TREES

On the outskirts of Lorrinel, Tom
paused to check the map on the
globe. The Silver Knight's trail came
to an end in the Forest of Fear.
A single word was written beneath
the tiny figure: *Noctila*.

"That sounds like a Beast's name,"
said Elenna.

"A new Beast? Then we have to

find the Silver Knight quickly,"
said Tom, putting the map away.
"We can't let him face a Beast
alone."

They galloped on until they reached
the edge of the Forest of Fear. "I don't
like the look of this," said Elenna.

Tom agreed. The tall trees grew so
close together he could barely see
ten paces into the gloom. A hundred
paces further along, a flock of birds
burst from the tree line, screeching
wildly. Tom spurred Storm towards
the commotion. A huge dark shadow
passed between the trees. A nasty
rotten smell reached Tom's
nostrils

The Varkule… Tom thought. "It's
here," he said, hand dropping to
the hilt of his sword.

The giant hyena flitted into the

undergrowth once more, disappearing out of sight.

"If it's not going to come out and fight, we have to go after it," said Tom.

"I'm with you," said Elenna.

Storm tossed his head as Tom steered him into the forest. Silver kept close to the stallion. "Easy, boy," said Tom. The air became cooler under the shelter of the trees. *Our first battle in the new Quest to save Avantia*, he thought.

Tom drew his sword, his eyes scanning the trees on both sides. Each cracking branch made him jerk his head. If the Varkule did attack, being mounted high on Storm would give him an advantage.

"There!" whispered Elenna, pointing to her left. Tom spurred

Storm in pursuit, leaping over a fallen trunk, as the Varkule crashed through the undergrowth ahead of them, its breath clouding the air.

Tom couldn't help but be impressed by the Varkule's tremendous power. It didn't slink between the trees, it smashed right through them, toppling saplings and snapping branches in its path.

"Duck!" said Elenna.

As Tom crouched over Storm's mane, an arrow from Elenna's bow whizzed past his ear, thudding into the Varkule's hind leg. The creature roared in pain and rolled over, careering into a tree with a mighty crack.

The Varkule scrambled onto its paws again and Tom charged. But the tree the Varkule had collided

with cracked and began to topple towards them. Silver howled and rushed to safety, and Tom yanked back on Storm's reins. The stallion's hooves wheeled in the air as the tree crashed down a fraction from them, showering Tom and Elenna with leaves and twigs. A hand span closer, and it would have broken Storm's neck.

As the air cleared of debris, the Varkule appeared on the other side, hackles bristling as it pawed the ground. Silver leapt through the air at the creature, but it tossed its massive head, and butted the wolf away. Silver scrambled up with a growl, but stayed back.

I have to get my friends out of harm's way, thought Tom. Jerking the reins around, he galloped Storm

away through the trees. He heard
a snarl and the pounding strides of
the Varkule as it came after them.
Suddenly, he could no longer feel
Elenna's hands gripping his waist.
Had she fallen?

Tom looked back. No – his friend
had managed to turn in the saddle,
gripping Storm with her knees. Both
hands steadied her bow and arrow.

"Keep going!" she yelled. "It's
gaining!"

Sure enough, as Tom urged Storm
on, he heard the Varkule tearing
through the trees, closing the gap.
He saw an overhanging branch
ahead. "Duck!" he called.

Leaning close to Storm's neck, he
felt the branch brush his hair. On
the other side, he looked back and
saw the Varkule smash through,

crunching the branch in his jaws and tossing it aside. Elenna was drawing her arrow back again, as Tom urged Storm on faster. He imagined at any moment feeling the giant hyena's claws raking down his back.

THRUM-THWACK!

"Got it!" Elenna cried.

Tom drew Storm to a halt and wheeled around. The Varkule lay on the ground, a deep groove of churned earth and broken foliage scarring the forest floor where it had tumbled. An arrow was lodged in its neck, and its flanks rose and fell with rapid breaths.

Tom felt no joy as he dismounted. "Time to put it out of its misery," he said, drawing his sword.

He was five paces from the Varkule when a glint in the tree above caught his eye. Gasping with shock, he stepped back and raised his shield, as the silver flash of a weapon plummeted down.

CHAPTER FIVE

MAN AND BEAST

The blow landed, shaking Tom's whole body and knocking him to his knees. He rolled out, away from the figure and found his feet. A man in gleaming silver armour stood before him, with a double-edged axe that glinted wickedly. He stood at least as tall as Taladon, broad-shouldered and straight-backed.

"I'm on your side," said Tom,

lowering his own sword. "My father Taladon is Master of the Beasts just like your leader, Tanner. I've brought the tokens you needed."

The Silver Knight strode forward, axe raised. Behind his visor, Tom saw the flash of fury in his dark eyes. The Knight swung his axe and Tom lifted his sword to counter the thunderous blow. The force almost drove him to his knees.

"Shall I shoot?" Elenna shouted.

Backing away, Tom glanced sideways and saw her with Storm and Silver, an arrow ready against her bowstring.

"Not yet!" Tom replied, deflecting another swipe, this one from the side and strong enough to slice him in two. Despite the plates of armour he wore, the Knight advanced more

quickly than any other Tom had seen,
dealing rapid strikes from every angle.
Tom parried and thrust with his
sword, but only to keep the Knight

at bay. He didn't want to kill his opponent unless he had to.

Instead he used the flat of the blade to strike the Knight's helmet with dull clangs.

Hopefully I can distract him, Tom thought.

Incredibly, the Silver Knight didn't seem to be getting tired, while Tom was already drawing ragged breaths. He stumbled backwards over a branch, and the Knight pressed his advantage. The first swipe sent Tom's shield spinning from his arm. The Knight followed the axe-blow with a punch that caught Tom in the ribs and tossed him through the air. He landed with a thud at the foot of a tree, and his sword arced out of sight.

"Wait!" he gasped. "Why are you doing this? Malvel is our foe!"

Again the Knight loomed over

Tom. For a moment, he seemed
to pause. *I'm getting through to him*,
Tom thought. But the Silver Knight
lifted the axe over his head in both
hands, ready to bring the blade
down into Tom's skull. As the blade
scythed down, Tom darted between
the Knight's legs. He heard the thud
as the axe-head lodged in the tree,
exactly where his head had been.

The Knight fought to free the blade.
Tom didn't have his sword or shield
so he ran shoulder-first, slamming
into the Knight's back. Pain exploded
through Tom's arm, but he caught
the Knight off-balance. The silver-
clad warrior slammed into the ground
with a clatter of armour. Tom jumped
on top of him, pinning the Knight
face down on the ground. The man
writhed beneath him like a wild horse.

"Help me hold him!" he shouted to Elenna.

In a heartbeat his friend had jumped onto the Knight's legs and pressed down with all her weight. Elenna struggled as he heaved beneath her. Gradually, the Knight stopped fighting and his head rested on the ground. Tom heard a deep voice whisper from beneath the

Knight's helmet: "So be it."

The Knight's head started to turn. And it didn't stop. Tom was horrified as the Silver Knight's helmet revolved around until the visor faced him.

"That's...impossible," gasped Elenna.

"No..." growled the Knight, as his visor lifted, revealing a handsome face beneath, with a dark, neatly trimmed beard. But his eyes were strange – his pupils were huge, his expression empty of life.

New strength seemed to surge through the body beneath Tom, as if every muscle was tense and pulsing. Tom was helpless as the Knight threw them both off and stood up.

"Malvel's cursed you," Tom said, grasping Elenna's hand to help her up. *This had to be the Evil Wizard's work!* "I don't know how he has done it, but you have to fight back. Don't give in. You're a Knight of Forton!"

The Knight's head turned again, with a hideous sound of creaking bones and stretching tendons. It rotated in a full circle while his shoulders and body remained motionless. It would have broken a normal person's neck, but Tom was beginning to understand the Silver Knight was no ordinary man.

As the head came back to face them, something had changed. Silver growled and Storm snorted in alarm.

Where the man's face had been, Tom saw thick grey feathers. A sharp yellow beak with a black tip had replaced his nose, and his eyes were wide circles of orange. Tom recognised the horrible face from the markings on the dragon-hide tomb.

"It's… It's an owl!" Elenna cried.

So this is what Aduro was afraid of…
Tom thought.

The Beast's mouth parted
impossibly wide, revealing a set of
slathering jaws lined with razor-sharp
teeth. Tom was frozen to the spot as
a voice emerged, hallway between
a squawk and a roar: "I am no Knight
of Forton! I am Noctila!"

CHAPTER SIX

OWL OF DEATH

The Silver Knight's armour morphed before Tom's eyes, sprouting grey feathers as the Beast's body swelled. It grew until its giant owl's head brushed the lowest tree branches. Its feet, which had been coated in armoured boots, changed to deadly silver claws, each the size of a cartwheel.

Tom backed towards Elenna. He saw his sword lying close to the Beast,

but where was his shield?

"I don't understand," said Elenna. "Aduro said the Knights conquered Beasts, not that they became Beasts themselves."

"That was in the past," roared the Knight-Beast. "You made me change! And now you will pay."

Tom searched desperately for his shield. "The Dark Wizard has cursed the Knights of Forton," he replied. Dread flooded him as he realised what they faced. If all six Knights turned into Beasts, it would be their hardest Quest yet.

Anger scorched his heart as he witnessed the depths of Malvel's evil. *He's turning once good men into enemies of the kingdom. Now the battle is really on!* Tom thought.

Noctila's transformation was

complete – the Beast was three times the size of the Silver Knight. The giant Owl-Beast spread her wings. Thick black liquid dripped from the tips, hissing as it landed on the ground. A noxious smell filled the air as the Beast climbed into the sky, breaking through the branches.

"It's burning tar!" Elenna said. "How will we even get close?"

Tom slapped Storm's rump. "Get away from here!" he shouted. The stallion obeyed, cantering off. Tom spotted his shield resting twenty paces away from his sword. Could he reach it before Noctila pounced? His sword was closer, but it wouldn't protect him against the deadly tar.

Noctila swept through the trees, wings dipped to slow her descent, and claws outstretched to tear their flesh apart. Tom ran for his sword, feeling the draft of the Beast bearing down behind him. He dived, snatching the sword in one hand and rolling back to his feet. With a desperate swipe, he fought back against the Beast's cruel talons, sending off a cascade of sparks.

Spots of poisonous, steaming tar landed all around him, filling the air with smoke. One drop hit the edge of his boot, melting the leather away. Tom grimaced in pain. He could only limp a few steps back before the Beast whirled in the air and raked her talons down the front of his tunic. He heard Elenna scream, as one talon caught in the material of his clothing and lifted him off the ground. He felt himself hurled aside, and thumped into a tree trunk, before sliding to the ground.

Tom shook his head, trying to catch
his breath. Through blurred vision
he saw Elenna and Silver fighting
side by side as the injured Varkule
dragged itself to face them, snapping

wildly and spraying them with flecks of spittle. Thankfully, Storm seemed to have made it to safety, because he was nowhere to be seen.

Get moving! Tom told himself.

Bleeding from his chest where Noctila's talons had caught him, Tom clambered up. He leant on the tree trunk for support. Somehow he'd managed to keep hold of his sword. His body felt like it was in another kingdom, and his vision was blurred. There were two Varkules, then four. He shook his head clear, lifting his sword to be ready for Noctila's next strike. But the Death Owl had disappeared, as silent as a shadow.

Tom heard a whine as brave Silver was swatted aside again and sent rolling into the undergrowth. The giant hyena snapped at Elenna with slavering jaws, pressing her back against a tree.

Tom limped weakly towards her, but another creature burst through the trees. Two powerful hind legs shot out and two iron-shod hooves smashed into the Varkule's temple. Storm!

The Varkule fell to the ground unconscious, as Elenna threw her arms around Storm's neck.

Tom hobbled to her side. Her eyes

widened when she saw his foot where Noctila's tar had eaten his boot away. "You're injured!"

"There'll be time to fix that later," said Tom, stroking Storm's mane. "Good kicking, friend."

Elenna peered up into the trees. "Where's Noctila?"

Before Tom could answer, a screech cut through the air, making the leaves rustle all around them. He heard the splintering of branches as Noctila fell from the sky, and landed in the centre of the clearing. The Beast's orange eyes narrowed when they spotted the fallen Varkule.

"She looks angry," muttered Elenna.

Tom pointed at the Beast. "Come and get me, Noctila!"

CHAPTER SEVEN

HELP FROM THE PLAINS

The Death Owl shook out her feathers and her beak split into something like an evil smile.

"Find a safe place to shoot from," said Tom. "I've got to reach my shield."

Elenna nodded, and they split up. Noctila's head swivelled from side to side, as though unsure of who she wanted to attack first. Tom darted

through the trees in a wide circuit
to where his shield rested beside the
bush, staying a safe distance from
the Beast's deadly dripping feathers.
Meanwhile, he saw Elenna expertly
climbing higher into the branches
of a large oak tree.

Noctila's glassy stare fixed on Tom
and she pounced. Tom drew up short
as the Beast landed just a few paces
away, blocking his route to his shield.
The Death Owl snapped her beak open
and closed, eager for a meal. She took
one step forward, flinching as an arrow
ricocheted off her beak. The Beast's
head snapped round angrily, as Elenna
shot again from her high position
astride a branch. This time Noctila
raised a wing – the arrow hit the
feathers and was scorched to ashes.

This is hopeless! Tom thought, as

another shaft burned on impact with the boiling tar. *We need help. A Beast's help.*

But to call one of the six Good Beasts, Tom needed his shield. *And I'll be burnt to a charred skeleton before I even get close!* he thought.

His hand fell to the belt at his waist, and he realised there just might be another way. Of the six jewels embedded in the leather, the ruby won from Torgor the Minotaur gave him the power to communicate with Beasts. But would it work over such distances? All the Good Beasts were several days' ride away…all except Tagus.

And we're running out of time…

Noctila drew back her protective wing and caught the next of Elenna's arrows in her jaws, crunching it to splinters. The Death Owl started to advance towards Tom's friend. How many arrows did she have left?

Tom clutched the ruby and faced northeast, towards the Central Plains. It was worth a try.

Hear me, Tagus, he willed. *We need you. Please!* He thought he felt the jewel become warm in his hand, but he couldn't be sure.

With Noctila's attention on Elenna, Tom saw a chance to recover his shield. Creeping forwards, he sneaked behind Noctila. But the Beast's pointed ears pricked up and she turned towards him with a half-twist of her head.

The Death Owl screeched and leapt at Tom, clawing the air, and sending down a shower of black tar. Tom dodged the falling droplets, abandoning his shield once more, and ran to the tree where Elenna was lodged. With the ground hissing and burning on all sides, he sheltered behind the massive trunk.

"We need to get out of the forest!" Elenna called down, as small fires spread around the base of the tree. "If the flames take hold, we'll be in trouble!"

Tom saw the panic in his friend's face, and he understood her fear. Elenna's parents had died in a forest fire.

"I know how you feel," Tom called up, "but this is the best place to be. If we go out in the open, Noctila can stalk us from the air – we'd have no chance."

Noctila screeched and clawed great clods of moss and earth with her talons. Her eyes narrowed to orange slits. Smoke curled around her as the undergrowth spluttered with flames. But the fire didn't seem to bother the Beast.

Sweat poured into Tom's eyes, making him squint and blink. His palm was slippery on the hilt of his sword.

Noctila strutted towards Storm and Silver. "Stop her!" begged Elenna.

At that moment, Tom felt the ground beneath his feet rumble. "Not another earthquake!" he muttered.

Storm snorted and stamped his hooves, and Noctila's head swivelled around almost a half-circle to stare at the far side of the clearing. The rumbling grew louder, and Tom felt the faint vibrations through his legs.

"What's she waiting for?" hissed Elenna.

That's not an earth tremor, Tom thought, a smile spreading over his lips. There was something repetitive about the sound, like a drum beat. *It's the sound of hooves.* He glanced up to Elenna. "Tagus is coming!"

Noctila stood her ground, ruffling her feathers. She looked triumphant.

A sense of deep unease twisted in Tom's gut like a blade. *Perhaps this was her plan all along... Have I drawn the Good Beast into a trap?*

CHAPTER EIGHT

A FIGHT IN FIRE

The low branches across the clearing burst apart, and Tagus cantered into view. He stood proudly, twice as tall as a man, his massive tawny chest rising and falling. His horse's flanks were slick with sweat and his powerful leg-muscles twitched from the gallop across the Plains. In his hand, he clutched a broadsword as long as a jousting lance. Tom knew no normal man would even be able to lift it. Tagus raised the blade towards Tom in a salute. Noctila hooted with what sounded like laughter, and paced towards where Storm and Silver sheltered beside a rotten, half-hollowed out trunk. Storm's eyes were wide with fear, and Silver cowered back, his teeth bared.

"Run!" Tom shouted to his animal companions.

Storm bolted further into the forest, and Silver darted in his wake. At the same moment, Tagus galloped across the clearing, swinging his sword to cut the Beast in two. Noctila's eyes swivelled to meet him. For a heartbeat, Tom thought Tagus's slash would connect, but the Owl-Beast sprung up into the air. Tagus's blade bit deep into the rotten trunk. As he

tried to free it, the great tree began to creak and lean. The Good Beast roared in pain as black steaming tar rained down from above, scattered by Noctila's beating wings.

"This isn't working," Elenna called, trying to line up another arrow. "While Noctila's in the air, she has the advantage."

Tom looked on, feeling helpless. They couldn't even get close to the Beast. Old dead leaves caught fire, and the flames seemed to leap from branch to branch, snatching at the tinder-dry wood. Angry red burns scarred Tagus's body, but he yanked his sword loose and reared on his hind hooves, jabbing and parrying Noctila's raking claws. Squawks of fury pierced Tom's eardrums, and he struggled to catch his breath in the thickening smoke. Through a patch of foliage, he saw Storm waiting. The loyal stallion hadn't run to safety at all.

What would I do without you? thought Tom.

The hulking tree popped and crackled as the fire found pockets of sap. It wouldn't be long before it collapsed, just like the tree that had almost crushed them earlier.

Maybe we can use it to help us! Tom thought. He grabbed Elenna's shoulder and pointed towards the bottom of the tree where Tagus's blade had cleaved the trunk. "A good shove should bring it down right on top of Noctila!" he said. "But it'll take both of us."

Elenna nodded, and they ran to the base of the tree. Noctila still hovered in the branches just out of reach, while Tagus tried desperately to strike home with his sword. Tom braced his hands against the trunk, and Elenna did the same. "Push!" Tom said, through gritted teeth.

As they strained, the huge tree seemed to give out an almost human-sounding groan, and the pale insides of the wood split open. Tom felt the trunk give and begin to topple. Noctila realised what was happening too late and shrieked as she was caught in the blazing foliage of the upper branches. Tom shielded his eyes as the tree crashed to the ground, engulfing the Owl-Beast.

Tagus lowered his sword and staggered to Tom's side. His hair was scorched away where Noctila's tar had fallen and part of his tail was

smouldering, but he seemed hardly
to notice his injuries.

"Thank you," said Tom.

The Good Beast dipped his head
in understanding.

"Is it over?" asked Elenna. Soot
stained her face. Silver had returned

to her side, pressing his body close to her legs. Storm tossed his mane as he emerged from his hiding place.

The fallen tree smoked, its branches were still. Nothing stirred beneath.

"The Beast must have been crushed," Tom said. He spotted his shield beside a trailing dead branch. As he went to fetch it, Tagus trotted slowly towards the smouldering tree. The Beast hobbled slightly from his injuries, his sword lowered at his side.

The blackened branches shifted.

"Get back!" shouted Tom, but it was too late.

A huge wing threw off a curtain of ash, and Noctila staggered upright. Her silver claws crunched over burnt wood. Patches of fire still burned over her body where flaming leaves clung to her feathers.

Tagus raised his sword again. But Tom could see the Beast was flagging. His injuries were taking their toll.

Whoosh!

With a vicious double flick of her wings, Noctila sprayed two arcs of burning tar in a loop around Tagus, encircling the Horse-Man and Tom's shield in a ring of fire. Tom had no choice but to back away from the baking wall of flame. Through the flickering barrier he saw Tagus startled, rearing wildly. He might be the brave Beast of the Plains, but when confronted with flames his animal instincts took over.

From Storm's frantic snorting, Tom realised his own steed was panicking too. He risked a glance back and saw Elenna crouched in the tree, her tunic pulled over her mouth to filter the smoke. Silver crouched at the base, unwilling to leave his mistress.

It's all going wrong! Tom cursed himself. *I brought Tagus here and now he's trapped. It won't be long before the smoke fills his lungs, and then....*

Tom clenched his fists and forced the despair from his mind. He needed his shield – it was the only thing that would protect them from the flames.

He rushed back to where Storm bucked and tossed his mane, seizing the reins.

"I need you now, brave friend," he muttered, patting his stallion's neck.

Storm stilled, and allowed Tom to climb into the saddle. Tom pulled the stallion's head around to face the climbing flames that entrapped Tagus.

"What are you doing?" shouted Elenna, her wide eyes very white in her soot-covered face.

Tom nodded towards Noctila, who hovered just above the clearing, daring Tom to try and pass. "Can you distract the Beast?" he asked. "You'll know when."

Elenna set her lips in a grim line, and deftly placed an arrow to her bowstring.

Tom dug his heels into Storm's flanks and the stallion sprang into a gallop straight towards the flames. Towards Noctila.

The Evil Beast lowered her talons, ready to snatch Tom from the saddle and tear him to pieces. Her wings drooled burning tar.

Tom pressed Storm on harder.

Just as they were about to reach the Beast, an arrow whipped through the air above Tom's head. Noctila jerked

upwards, drawing her wings closed to block the shaft. Tom charged through the gap.

The wall of flames reared taller than Tom's head. He'd never leapt a fence so high before, but he knew Storm wouldn't shy away. He waited as late as possible, until the heat became unbearable. Then he yanked back on the reins.

Storm leapt towards the wall of fire.

If this doesn't work, Tom thought, *we're all going to die...*

CHAPTER NINE

DEATH KNELL

Tom threw his weight forward in the saddle. Ash-filled air streamed through Storm's mane and into Tom's eyes as waves of heat blasted them from below.

Storm's hooves slammed back into the ground on the other side of the fire wall. Tom was almost thrown from his stallion's back, and blinked the tears of smoke from his eyes.

"We made it!" he cried.

They'd landed beside Tagus, who paced around the outside of the fire ring, looking desperately for an escape. Tom dismounted, and snatched up his shield.

"It's all right," he shouted to the Good Beast. "I can get us out of this."

He held his shield towards the climbing fires, willing the power of Ferno's scale to work its magic – the token from the Fire Dragon repelled flames. At once, it was if a powerful wind was blowing, ripping open an archway in the orange, flickering wall. The heat on Tom's face cooled.

Sheltering close behind the wood, he made his way through the gap. But when he glanced behind, he saw Storm and Tagus standing beside each other. Neither moved.

They're still afraid, he thought.
Their instincts are taking over.

"You can do it!" he called back.
The shield was already starting to
shake on his arm. If they didn't come
soon, he'd lose the strength to keep
the fire at bay.

Storm stamped the ground, but
still held back.

"I won't let you come to harm!"
Tom urged. Storm snorted, and took
a small step forward. "That's it!"
shouted Tom. "Follow me!"

Storm broke into a trot, and Tom
took another step, so he was standing
directly under the opened arch. The
flames swirled in strange patterns
around him, driven back by the
powerful magic of the dragon's scale.
Still, he felt the heat crawling over
his skin and singeing his hair.

"Quickly!" he urged.

To Tom's relief, Tagus followed in
Storm's wake, dipping his head as he
passed beneath the doorway. Tom
waited until he was sure his friends
were safe, and then dove through
himself, rolling across the forest floor.
He saw the flames fall like curtains,
closing up the space.

He found his feet, as a silent shadow fell over him. Noctila swooped down, talons outstretched. Tom jerked aside, unable to draw his sword in time, and smashed his shield into the side of the Beast's jabbing beak. Noctila shrieked as she tumbled sideways.

"So you're not invincible!" Tom shouted.

The Beast slammed into a tree, and Tom heard a scream from above. Elenna, disturbed by the impact, was dangling from a branch. Tom watched in horror as she lost her grip and tumbled through leaves and branches. She landed in a heap at the bottom.

Right beside Noctila.

Tom leapt forwards to protect his friend, but Tagus was quicker. He thrust out a double-kick with his front hooves, sending Noctila

staggering awkwardly backwards.
As the Horse-Man followed up with
a swinging sword, Tom rushed to
Elenna's side. She sat up, rubbing her
head, and Silver nuzzled at her side,
whining anxiously.

"Are you hurt?" Tom asked.

"Not badly," she replied. The roars
of Tagus and the angry hoots of
Noctila filled the air. "This Beast is
unstoppable!" she added.

An idea hit Tom. The tokens!
"Maybe not," he said.

He reached up to fish inside Storm's
saddlebag, and then drew out the
net. The silver webbing sparkled. Tom
could tell, even though it was almost
as light as gossamer, it was strong as
any rope. "We could use this to stop
the Beast," he said, "but we'll need
to work together."

Tom glanced to where Tagus and the Death Owl were engaging in battle. Noctila snarled and sprayed fire. But Tagus would only retreat a few steps before resuming his attack.

Tom seized Elenna's arm and pulled her after him away from the fight. They headed towards two trees that stood ten paces apart on the far side of the clearing. "Lay the net out between us," Tom said. Elenna understood his plan at once and did as he asked. They each stood behind a tree, hidden from Tagus and Noctila. The net was almost invisible on the ground.

Tom gripped the ruby once again, and focused his mind. *Tagus, hear me*, he thought. *You have to bring Noctila this way…*

Peering out from the trunk, he saw Tagus respond at once, retreating towards their position, still lunging with his sword to keep the Beast at bay. Noctila's orange eyes gleamed with hatred as she pursued him.

It's working, Tom thought.

Tagus swivelled on his hooves, away from the Beast, and galloped towards the net. Noctila thrust into the air, and swooped after him.

"Get ready!" Tom mouthed to Elenna.

Noctila closed on Tagus, her beak glinting with the remaining fires. Tom worried for a moment that she might actually catch the Horse-Man, gripping his neck and wringing his life away. But Tagus found a reserve of strength and thundered past them.

"Now!" shouted Tom.

He and Elenna threw the net into the air, and the Death Owl hurtled into the mesh. The force of the Beast almost yanked Tom's arms from their sockets. He heard Elenna cry out as they were both heaved off their feet.

"Keep hold!" yelled Tom. "Don't let the Beast escape!"

But to his surprise, once Noctila hit the ground, the Death Owl didn't struggle. There were no flames

bursting from her feathers, and the only sound she gave was a feeble hoot. Tom gripped his edge of the net tightly, and stared. The Beast's head swivelled to face them, her beak gaping as if she was drowning. Her eyes changed from angry orange to yellow. Tom gasped as the Death Owl's body shrank, and her feathers began to harden to something like metal. Her beak fell away to reveal the handsome face of a man.

In less than five breaths, the Beast had become a Knight again, clothed from head to toe in silver armour. Still clutching the net, Tom crouched beside the fallen warrior. The warrior's breastplate rose and fell in shallow breaths and he stared at Tom with pale eyes. They contained no shred of hate or evil.

"Are you all right?" Tom asked.

The Knight's lips spread into a grateful smile, then parted as if he was about to speak. But his body began to fade like breaking mist. Before he could utter a word, he vanished. The silver net disappeared too, leaving Tom's fingers holding nothing but air.

"Have we killed him?" Elenna muttered.

"I don't think so," Tom replied. "He looked happy. I suppose we've freed him from his curse, so he can—"

A clapping sound made Tom spin around, his hand dropping to his sword-hilt. A man stood in the shadow of the trees.

Tom swallowed back his dread.

He'd never thought he would see that face again.

CHAPTER TEN

ENEMY OF AVANTIA

"Malvel!" Tom said, drawing his sword.

"So you remember me?" said the Evil Wizard. "How flattering!"

Tom took a step forwards, shielding Elenna, and pointed his blade at Malvel. "I don't know how you're here, but you won't be here for long. Take out your weapon."

"Save the speeches, boy," Malvel spat.

"Now isn't the time you'll face me."

As the wizard stepped from the gloom, Tom saw that something wasn't right. Though Malvel wore a dark, simple cloak, he seemed to glide above the ground, rather than walk.

"It's just a vision," Tom said.

Malvel's body was surrounded by the faintest flickering of blue, like a shield.

"The Eternal Flame!" Elenna gasped. "You're still in the fire from Seraph."

"Clever girl!" said Malvel. "I may be imprisoned in the Flame, but I'm not in Seraph. I'm in Gorgonia, to be exact – my former kingdom. I can't say it's pleasant in this fiery cage, but it's only temporary."

"What do you mean?" asked Tom, circling the apparition. "Even your

magic isn't powerful enough to break the spell of the Flame."

Malvel arched an eyebrow. "Perhaps not my magic, but you will see soon enough how I mean to return."

The Evil Wizard's words sent a shiver down Tom's spine, but he managed a grim smile. *He's just trying to frighten me*, he thought.

Malvel cast an arm around the smouldering forest. "It seems my first little surprise caused you some bother," he sneered.

"Nothing we couldn't get the better of," Elenna replied.

"Really?" said Malvel. "Well, there are five more for you to 'get the better of' – or not. At this very moment they're on their way to the five corners of the kingdom."

Tom felt hope seep from his heart. His suspicions were right: the Knights weren't here to protect the kingdom; they'd come to destroy it.

"Avantia won't fall while we stand," he shouted.

Malvel pointed to Tagus, whose body was covered with scars and burns. "Your other Beast friends might not get off so lightly. Do you really have five more battles like this in you?"

"While there's blood in my veins," Tom said, "I'll fight whatever evil crosses my path, whether it's five battles or a hundred."

The vision of Malvel floated closer, within a sword-length of Tom. Cruel lines etched his face. "You've said your piece, now I'll say mine. Pushing me into the Eternal Flame was the best thing you could have done. I will return to Avantia, and when I do, I'm going to take everything you hold dear and crush it within my fist. You will beg to die before I kill you, Tom."

The blue fire darkened, dimming Malvel's image inside. From the bottom up, it seeped away like a smoke column snatched by the wind. The Evil Wizard's head was the last part to vanish.

As it did, Tom saw that he was smiling.

A stiff breeze toyed with the branches of the trees and brought gooseflesh up across Tom's skin.

"Don't listen to his threats," said Elenna. "Malvel is trapped. Aduro told us so."

Tom inspected the blade of his sword grimly, still sharp after so many battles. "All we can do is be ready," he said. He sheathed the sword at his hip and strode towards Storm.

"Don't you need to rest?" asked Elenna.

Tom unfastened Storm's saddlebag and drew out the magical globe-map. "There's no time," he said. "Let's see where our Quest takes us next."

Join Tom on the next stage
of the Beast Quest when he meets

SHAMANI
THE RAGING
FLAME

Win an exclusive
Beast Quest T-shirt and goody bag!

In every Beast Quest book the Beast Quest logo is
hidden in one of the pictures. Find the logos in books
55 to 60 and make a note of which pages they appear
on. Write the six page numbers on a postcard and
send it in to us.
Each month we will draw one winner to receive
a Beast Quest T-shirt and goody bag.

THE BEAST QUEST COMPETITION:
THE MASTER OF THE BEASTS
Orchard Books
338 Euston Road, London NW1 3BH
Australian readers should email:
childrens.books@hachette.com.au

New Zealand readers should write to:
Beast Quest Competition
4 Whetu Place, Mairangi Bay, Auckland, NZ
or email: childrensbooks@hachette.co.nz

Only one entry per child.
Final draw: 4 March 2013

You can also enter this competition
via the Beast Quest website: www.beastquest.co.uk

Join the Quest,
Join the Tribe

www.beastquest.co.uk

Have you checked out the Beast Quest website?
It's the place to go for games, downloads, activities,
sneak previews and lots of fun!

You can read all about your favourite Beasts, down-
load free screensavers and desktop wallpapers for
your computer, and even challenge your friends
to a Beast Tournament.

Sign up to the newsletter at www.beastquest.co.uk
to receive exclusive extra content and the oppor-
tunity to enter special members-only competitions.
We'll send you up-to-date info on all the Beast
Quest books, including the next exciting series
which features six brand-new Beasts!

Get 30% off all Beast Quest Books at www.beastquest.co.uk
Enter the code BEAST at the checkout.

Offer valid in UK and ROI, offer expires December 2013

FREE COLLECTOR CARDS INSIDE!

Series 10: MASTER OF THE BEASTS
COLLECT THEM ALL!

An old enemy has come back to haunt Tom –
and unleash six awesome new Beasts!

978 1 40831 518 7

978 1 40831 519 4

978 1 40831 520 0

978 1 40831 521 7

978 1 40831 522 4

978 1 40831 523 1

Series 11: THE NEW AGE
Out September 2012

Meet six terrifying new Beasts!

Elko Lord of the Sea
Tarrok the Blood Spike
Brutus the Hound of Horror
Flaymar the Scorched Blaze
Serpio the Slithering Shadow
Tauron the Pounding Fury

Watch out for the next
Special Bumper
Edition
OUT OCT 2012!

SPECIAL BUMPER EDITION!

The Chronicles of Avantia

FROM THE DARK, A HERO ARISES...

Dare to enter the kingdom of Avantia.

A new evil arises in Avantia. Lord Derthsin has ordered his armies into the four corners of Avantia. If the four Beasts of Avantia can find their Chosen Riders they might have the strength to challenge Derthsin. But if they fail, the land of Avantia will be lost forever...

FIRST HERO, CHASING EVIL CALL TO WAR, FIRE AND FURY-OUT NOW!

www.chroniclesofavantia.com